This book
BELONGS
to
....

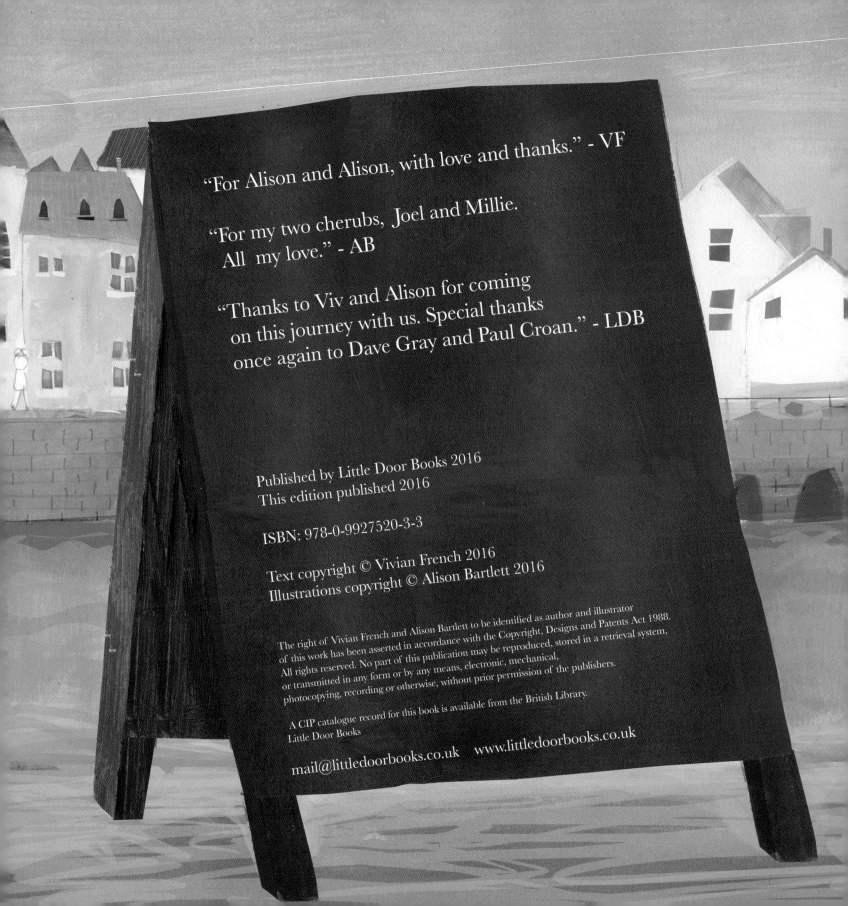

"For Alison and Alison, with love and thanks." - VF

"For my two cherubs, Joel and Millie.
All my love." - AB

"Thanks to Viv and Alison for coming
on this journey with us. Special thanks
once again to Dave Gray and Paul Croan." - LDB

Published by Little Door Books 2016
This edition published 2016

ISBN: 978-0-9927520-3-3

Text copyright © Vivian French 2016
Illustrations copyright © Alison Bartlett 2016

Little Door Books

mail@littledoorbooks.co.uk   www.littledoorbooks.co.uk

Captain Cranko & Seadog Steve

Vivian French   Alison Bartlett

Captain Crankie lived by the sea.
Every day he and Seadog Steve
went out in the Mary Rose,
taking visitors and villagers to watch
the dolphins and the seals.

Every evening they came home and ate their tea together ...

and after tea Captain Crankie washed up,
and Seadog Steve put the dishes away.
They liked things tidy. But the villagers weren't tidy at all.

Little Sammy Smith left his old tin bucket
lying in the road ...

Big Billy Bragg hid his broken skate board under a bench ...

Mr and Mrs Walls threw their old umbrellas
into their front garden ...

and there they stayed.

"This won't do!" said Captain Crankie.
"It won't do at all!"
"Woof!" agreed Seadog Steve,

and they heaved and they hauled and they pushed and they pulled the rubbish all the way back to their own house ...

and loaded it into the Mary Rose.

Chug chug chug!

Out to sea they went.

Chug chug chug!

SPLASH!

Into the deep dark sea went the rubbish.

Down,
down,
down,
it sank ...

Captain Crankie smiled.
"There!" he said. "A job well done!"
And he and Seadog Steve
went chugging back to the harbour,
went to bed, and snored
peacefully till morning.

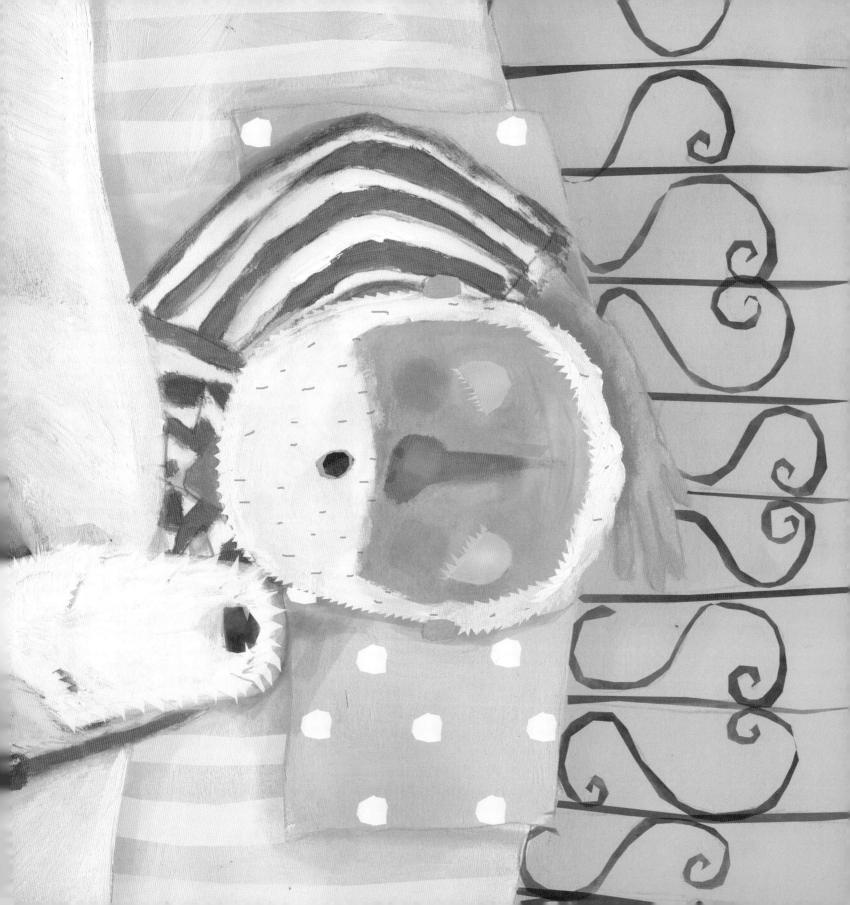

The next week there was more rubbish.
Old Granny Greenhill dumped her
shopping trolley near a tree ...

Betty the butcher's wife
tossed a three-legged chair into a ditch ...

Harry Hopkins carried his old car tyre
down to the beach ... and there they stayed.

"This won't do!" said Captain Crankie.
"It won't do at all!"

"Woof!" agreed Seadog Steve.
And off they went to tidy up,
and take the rubbish out to sea.

Under the waves the rubbish was spreading.
"This won't do!" said little mermaid Millie. "It won't do at all!"

"Arf!" agreed the seals, and the dolphins
nodded their big grey heads.
"I must speak to Captain Crankie!" said Millie.

The very next evening Captain Crankie
and Seadog Steve had a big surprise ...

a little mermaid was sitting on a rock by the harbour wall.

"Hello," said Millie. "That's a lot of rubbish in your boat."

"Yes," said Captain Crankie. "People in our village are VERY untidy!"

"H'mmmm … " said Millie.
"I need to show you something. Come with me!"
So Captain Crankie put on his bathing suit,
and Seadog Steve put on his water wings.

"This way!" said Millie, and she dived into the water. Captain Crankie and Seadog Steve dived after her.

Down ...
down ...

down ... down they swam

to the bottom of the sea.

"There!"
said Millie.

"Look at all that rubbish!"

"Oh dear," said Captain Crankie. "This won't do! It won't do at all!"

"Exactly," said Millie. "What are you going to do about it?"

"H'mmmm ..." said Captain Crankie.

"Woof!" said Seadog Steve.

"Very clever! said Captain Crankie,
and he whispered to Millie, and she whispered to the seals, and they
whispered to the dolphins ... and Captain Crankie and Seadog Steve
swam back to the Mary Rose.

The next day Captain Crankie
put up a new sign.

And all the villagers came hurrying out.

But they didn't catch fish ...
Not at all! They each caught something VERY special!

"I'll plant
a red geranium!"
said Granny Greenhill.

"Perfect for a shelf!"
said Mr Walls.

"I can wheel
my shopping home,"
said Betty.

"Woof!" said Seadog Steve.
Captain Crankie smiled.

"There's a use
for everything!
Now, let's go home for
toast and tea ..."

And as the Mary Rose chugged
back to harbour, Millie sat on her
rock and waved them goodbye.